The Falcon Rising

Yugesh Kumar

Published by Sukhminder Singh, 2023.

THE FALCON RISING

First edition. July 20, 2023.

ISBN: 979-8223242468

Written by Yugesh Kumar.

Table of Contents

Disclaimer:

The following is a disclaimer for the book titled "The Falcon Rising." Please read this disclaimer carefully before engaging with the content of this book.

Content: "The Falcon Rising" is a work of fiction. All characters, events, and incidents portrayed in this book are products of the author's imagination. Any resemblance to actual persons, living or dead, or real- life events is purely coincidental.

Sensitivity: This book may contain elements and themes that some readers may find sensitive or triggering. It may include violence, action sequences, suspenseful situations, and intense emotional experiences. Reader discretion is advised, and individuals are encouraged to assess their personal comfort level before engaging with the content.

Accuracy: While the author has made every effort to ensure the accuracy of information and details presented in this book, historical, geographical, or factual inaccuracies may exist. The book should be enjoyed primarily as a work of fiction and not as a reliable source of information.

Endorsement: The views, opinions, and beliefs expressed by characters in this book are fictional and do not necessarily reflect those of the author or the publisher.

Reader Responsibility: The author and the publisher shall not be held responsible for any personal interpretations, actions, or consequences derived from the reader's engagement with this book. It is the responsibility of the reader to exercise their own judgment and discretion while interpreting and applying the content.

Copyright: "The Falcon Rising" and all its original content are the intellectual property of the author. No part of this book may be reproduced, distributed, or transmitted in any form or by any means without the written permission of the author.

By engaging with the content of "The Falcon Rising," readers acknowledge and accept the terms outlined in this disclaimer.

Please note that this disclaimer is subject to change without notice. It is recommended to refer back to the latest version of the disclaimer available in the book.

Thank you for your understanding and cooperation.

Preface:

In the depths of darkness, when the world trembles under the weight of injustice, a beacon of hope emerges. A

symbol of strength and freedom, soaring high above the troubled land, casting its shadow upon the hearts of the oppressed. This is the tale of "The Falcon Rising."

Within the pages that follow, you will embark on a journey through a world gripped by corruption and despair. But fear not, for this is not a tale of despair alone. It is a tale of resilience, of unwavering determination, and the indomitable spirit that resides within the hearts of ordinary individuals who dare to rise against the odds.

"The Falcon Rising" introduces us to a protagonist who discovers a hidden truth, a truth that alters the course of their existence. Inspired by the legendary Falcon, a symbol of unwavering justice, the protagonist embarks on a quest to follow in the Falcon's footsteps, to embrace the mantle of a hero. In the face of relentless adversaries and rising threats, our protagonist undergoes a transformative journey. They delve into the depths of their own being, honing their skills, both physical and mental, to become a force to be reckoned with. They seek allies, form bonds, and navigate the treacherous waters of trust and betrayal.

Through epic battles, the protagonist confronts the embodiment of evil, a formidable antagonist whose dark ambitions threaten to shatter the fragile peace. The culmination of their struggle unfolds in a climactic clash, where their very beliefs and the essence of the Falcon's legacy are put to the ultimate test.

"The Falcon Rising" is a testament to the power of unity, the strength of conviction, and the enduring human spirit. It is a tale that reminds us that even in our darkest moments, we can rise above the shadows, fueled by the unwavering resolve to fight for what is right.

As you turn the pages of this book, immerse yourself in a world teeming with action, suspense, and profound emotion. Witness the rise of a hero, feel the pulse of their journey, and be swept away by the triumphs and tribulations that shape their destiny.

May "The Falcon Rising" inspire you, dear reader, to find the Falcon within yourself, to soar above adversity, and to believe in the power of hope, for it is through the collective efforts of courageous souls that the world finds its salvation.

Embrace the call to rise, for the Falcon awaits.

Chapter 1: Introduction

In the breathtaking world of "The Falcon Rising," a novel that will sweep you away into a realm of adventure and destiny, two ancient and noble families find themselves entangled in a conflict that spans generations. Filled with intrigue, courage, and an unyielding desire for justice, this epic tale follows the remarkable journey of Patrick, a member of the esteemed White Falcons family, and Ella, a strong-willed woman with a connection to the Black Falcons.

Patrick, our captivating main character, hails from a lineage steeped in tradition and honor. As a descendant of the legendary White Falcons, he possesses an innate talent for falconry, a skill that has been passed down through generations. Patrick's love for the majestic birds of prey not only defines his identity but also fuels his relentless pursuit of truth and justice.

Ella, a fiery and independent woman, emerges as the second main character, capturing the hearts of readers with her fierce determination and unwavering loyalty. Raised within the Black Falcons family, she has been molded by their proud heritage and holds a deep sense of responsibility to protect her lineage's secrets and reputation. Ella's elder brother, Rodriguez

, stands as a steadfast companion, while Alberto, another member of the Black Falcons, becomes an unexpected ally whose loyalties are tested throughout their journey.

As the worlds of the White Falcons and Black Falcons collide, long-standing rivalries resurface, ancient

prophecies come to light, and the true nature of honor and sacrifice is revealed. Patrick and Ella find themselves thrust into a dangerous quest, where they must unravel the mysteries of their shared past and confront the dark forces that threaten their families' legacies.

Within the pages of "The Falcon Rising," readers will embark on an extraordinary adventure, where courage and determination are their compasses, and the bonds of friendship and love become their guiding light. Prepare to be captivated by the rich tapestry of this world, where falcons soar through the skies, destinies intertwine, and the strength of one's spirit can change the course of history.

Introduce the protagonist, their background, and their motivation.

In the heart of "The Falcon Rising," our protagonist Patrick emerges as a character shaped by a deep- rooted legacy and a burning desire for justice. Born into the esteemed White Falcons family, Patrick carries the weight of their ancient traditions and values upon his shoulders. From an early age, he was initiated into the intricate art of falconry, learning the delicate balance between strength and grace that mirrored his family's ethos.

Patrick's background is one of privilege, but it is his unwavering commitment to upholding justice that truly defines him. The legacy of his ancestors fuels his motivation to become a force for good in a world plagued by darkness and corruption. He sees himself as a protector, not only of his family but also of the innocent and vulnerable.

With every flight of his falcon and every connection forged with these magnificent creatures, Patrick deepens his bond to the natural world, finding solace and purpose in their company. Through his unique skillset, he gains an unparalleled perspective, navigating the skies with grace and precision. It is through the eyes of his avian companions that Patrick sees the world with unwavering clarity, always seeking the truth and defending those who cannot defend themselves.

However, Patrick's motivation extends beyond personal ambition. In a world where the Black Falcons, a rival family, have their own secrets and agendas, Patrick is driven to uncover the truth that has long remained hidden. He yearns to break free from the constraints of ancestral feuds and forge a path of unity, where the bonds of family and loyalty transcend the divisions of the past.

Set the stage for the world in which the story takes place.

In "The Falcon Rising," the stage is set in a world both familiar and enchanting, where the skies echo with the graceful flight of majestic falcons and ancient families hold the key to long-standing secrets. It is a realm where tradition intertwines with mysticism, and honor binds the very fabric of society.

The story unfolds in a land rich with diverse landscapes, from rolling hills and dense forests to towering mountains and vast open plains. Nature, with its untamed beauty, serves as a backdrop for the unfolding drama, reflecting the untamed spirit that courses through the veins of its inhabitants.

Within this world, two noble families hold prominence: the White Falcons and the Black Falcons. These families are not only distinguished by their shared lineage but also by their unique connection to the falcons that soar above them. The White Falcons, known for their unwavering loyalty and adherence to a strict code of honor, find solace and guidance in the skies, bonding closely with their falcon companions.

Conversely, the Black Falcons, shrouded in mystery and secrecy, possess an air of intrigue, their falcons representing an enigma waiting to be unraveled.

Amidst the grandeur of the land, a sense of history and mythology permeates every corner. Ancient prophecies whisper in the wind, foretelling a great destiny that will unfold. Legends of heroes and villains, battles fought, and victories won echo through the annals of time, shaping the present and setting the stage for the future.

Yet, it is not only the natural and mystical elements that define this world but also the people who inhabit it. From bustling cities teeming with life and diversity to secluded villages nestled in remote corners, a tapestry of cultures and traditions weaves itself into the fabric of society. These vibrant communities, with their unique customs and beliefs, provide a rich tapestry of characters who will play their parts in the unfolding tale.

As the story progresses, the reader will be immersed in the intricate tapestry of this world, where the beauty of nature, the weight of history, and the clash of falcon families converge. It is within this realm that the protagonist, Patrick, and his companions embark on a journey that will test their resolve, challenge their convictions, and ultimately shape the destiny of their world.

Chapter 2: The Call to Adventure

The sun began its ascent, casting a golden hue across the vast landscape. Patrick stood at the edge of the precipice, his gaze fixed on the horizon. The morning air carried a whisper, a call that tugged at his heart and beckoned him towards an unknown destiny. He felt the weight of his family's legacy pressing upon him, urging him to answer the call, to embark on the adventure that awaited.

The previous night, as the moon bathed the world in its ethereal glow, Patrick had a vision. A falcon, resplendent in its white plumage, soared through his dreams, its piercing eyes filled with purpose. The vision had filled him with a mixture of awe and trepidation, for he knew that such visions were never mere happenstance. They were the threads woven by fate, threads that could unravel destinies and forge new paths.

With resolute determination, Patrick turned away from the precipice and descended the rugged path that led to the heart of his family's estate. The sprawling grounds, adorned with towering trees and elegant falcon perches, greeted him. It was a sanctuary where falcons and humans coexisted, a testament to the bond that generations had cultivated.

In the distance, Patrick spotted his mentor, Elder Farin, a wise and weathered figure whose face bore the marks of countless seasons. With a nod of recognition, Patrick approached, his heart racing with anticipation.

"Elder Farin," Patrick called out respectfully. "I have received a vision, a sign from the falcons. It is as if they are calling me to a greater purpose."

The elder's gaze met Patrick's, his eyes reflecting both understanding and caution. "Visions are not to be taken lightly, young Patrick," he replied, his voice carrying the weight of wisdom. "They are the messages of the spirits, guiding us towards the paths we must tread. Tell me, what did this vision reveal to you?"

Patrick recounted his dream, the majestic falcon that had seemed to transcend the boundaries of the physical world, its wings carrying it towards an unknown destination. As he spoke, Elder Farin listened intently, his expression growing increasingly grave.

"The falcon has always been our guide, our symbol of nobility and vigilance," the elder mused. "If it has appeared to you, young Patrick, it is a sign that you are chosen. The time has come for you to heed the call and embark on a journey of great importance."

Patrick's heart quickened at the elder's words, a mix of excitement and uncertainty coursing through his veins. "What is this journey, Elder Farin? Where will it lead me?"

The elder's gaze held a mix of sympathy and resolve. "I cannot provide all the answers, for destiny reveals its secrets in due time. But I can tell you this: your path will intertwine with another, someone whose destiny is entwined with yours. Together, you will face trials and tribulations, uncovering truths that have long been concealed."

Patrick's mind swirled with questions, yet he knew that the elder's words held a profound truth. It was time to step beyond the boundaries of his family's estate, to embrace the unknown and forge a new narrative for himself and those he would encounter on his journey.

As the sun climbed higher in the sky, Patrick took a deep breath, steeling himself for the adventure that lay ahead. He would gather his falcon, his loyal companion and guide, and set forth on a path that would test his courage, challenge his beliefs, and shape his destiny.

With each step he took, Patrick embraced the call to adventure, knowing that he would never be the same again. The falcons' message echoed in his heart, a reminder that greatness awaited those who dared to soar beyond the confines of familiarity. And so, with resolve burning in his eyes, Patrick began his journey, ready to meet the one whose fate would intertwine with his, ready to embark on a quest that would change their lives and the destiny of the falcon families forever.

The protagonist receives a mysterious message or encounter that changes their life.

In the depths of the night, when the world slumbered, Patrick found himself awakened by an otherworldly presence. A soft breeze rustled through his chamber, carrying a whisper that seemed to emanate from the very air itself. Intrigued and alert, he rose from his bed, following the ethereal voice that beckoned him.

As he stepped into the moonlit courtyard, his eyes were drawn to a figure standing amidst the shadows. The figure was cloaked in darkness, yet a radiant aura surrounded them, casting a pale glow on their face. Patrick's heart raced as he approached, a mixture of curiosity and trepidation swelling within him.

"Who are you?" Patrick asked, his voice barely above a whisper.

The mysterious figure inclined their head, their voice carrying a haunting melody. "I am the Harbinger, the messenger of fate and transformation. I have come to bestow upon you a burden and a blessing, for you, Patrick, have been chosen for a destiny that will shape the course of our world."

Patrick's breath caught in his throat as he absorbed the weight of the Harbinger's words. His life would never be the same again. The encounter, shrouded in enigma, carried with it the promise of purpose and the weight of responsibility.

The Falcon, a legendary figure, is introduced as a symbol of hope and justice.

Legend whispered through the land of a mythical being known as the Falcon, a figure whose name echoed with tales of courage and righteousness. It was said that the Falcon had emerged during times of great darkness, spreading its wings to cast light upon the shadows and restore balance to a troubled world. The symbol of the Falcon resonated deeply within Patrick, reminding him of the ideals he held dear. The stories of its grace and unwavering dedication to justice fueled his spirit, igniting a flame within his heart. The Falcon became more than a mere legend—it became a beacon of hope, a symbol of the values he sought to embody.

The protagonist is inspired to follow in the Falcon's footsteps and fight for what is right.

In the wake of the encounter with the Harbinger and the resurgence of the Falcon's legend, Patrick felt a newfound determination surging through his veins. The mysterious message had stirred something deep within him, awakening a fervent desire to fight for what was right, to be a force for justice in a world tainted by darkness.

Patrick resolved to follow in the Falcon's footsteps, to be a guardian of the innocent and a champion of the downtrodden. He understood the immense challenges that lay ahead, the sacrifices that would be required, but he was undeterred. The weight of his family's legacy and the call of destiny propelled him forward, fueling his every step.

With each passing day, Patrick's training intensified. He honed his skills with the falcons, forging an unbreakable bond with his feathered companions. As he soared through the skies, his falcon by his side, he embraced the essence of the Falcon, embodying the virtues of hope, justice, and unwavering determination.

Inspired by the legendary figure and guided by the mysterious encounter, Patrick vowed to dedicate his life to the pursuit of truth and the restoration of harmony. The path would be arduous, fraught with trials and adversaries, but he knew deep within his heart that he was destined to make a difference.

And so, with the spirit of the Falcon burning bright within him, Patrick embarked on his quest, ready to face the challenges that awaited him. His resolve would be tested, his faith in his purpose pushed to its limits, but he would not falter. For he had been chosen, touched by fate and entrusted with the power to reshape the world, one righteous act at a time.

In the realm of the White Falcons, the air crackled with anticipation as Patrick delved deeper into his training. The walls of the ancient training ground echoed with the fluttering of wings and the whispers of knowledge passed down through generations. It was within these hallowed halls that Patrick would undergo a metamorphosis, both physically and spiritually.

Under the watchful eye of Elder Farin, Patrick immersed himself in the rigors of falconry. From dawn till dusk, he sparred with his avian companions, honing his reflexes, and sharpening his senses. His body became an extension of the falcon's grace, his movements fluid and precise.

But the training extended far beyond physical prowess. Elder Farin recognized that true power lay not only in the strength of the body but also in the depths of the mind and the purity of the spirit. Patrick was taught the ancient ways of connecting with the falcons on a profound level, delving into the realms of telepathy and empathy, forging a bond that transcended the boundaries of the physical.

Days turned into weeks, and weeks into months as Patrick absorbed the wisdom imparted by his mentor. The falcons became his companions, their keen intellect guiding him on a path of self-discovery.

Through their eyes, he witnessed the world from a different perspective, a perspective that demanded both vigilance and compassion.

As Patrick trained, a transformation unfolded within him. He shed the uncertainty that had once plagued his steps, replacing it with unwavering confidence and a heightened awareness of the world around him. His senses became keener, his intuition sharper. He could discern the hidden truths that lay beneath the surface, sensing the intentions of others and unraveling the webs of deception.

Yet, it was not only his skills that underwent a transformation. Patrick's spirit blossomed, infused with the virtues of the Falcon. He became a beacon of hope, a source of inspiration for his fellow White Falcons and those who witnessed his dedication.

They saw in him the embodiment of the legends, a reminder that righteousness and courage could triumph over the darkest of adversities.

In the stillness of the night, as Patrick communed with his falcon companion, he felt the weight of his purpose settle upon him. The training had not only shaped his abilities but also instilled within him a profound understanding of his role in the world. He

was destined to be a guardian, a protector of the innocent, and a symbol of justice.

With newfound clarity, Patrick emerged from his training, ready to face the challenges that awaited him beyond the walls of the White Falcons' domain. His transformation was not only physical but also a testament to his unwavering resolve to fight for what was right, to follow the path set before him by the Falcon and the mysterious encounter that had changed his life.

The time had come for Patrick to spread his wings and soar beyond the sheltered embrace of his training ground. The world awaited, its complexities and perils ready to test his mettle. He was no longer the wide- eyed novice but a warrior, emboldened by his training and infused with the spirit of the Falcon.

And so, with his falcon companion by his side, Patrick embarked on the next chapter of his journey, the echoes of his training reverberating within him. The trials would be arduous, and the path ahead uncertain, but his transformation had equipped him with the strength and wisdom to navigate the challenges that lay ahead.

As the sun dipped below the horizon, Patrick spread his wings, ready to soar into the unknown. The world awaited its champion, its guardian of justice and hope. And Patrick, armed with his falcon and the teachings of the White Falcons, would rise to meet the challenges head-on, embracing the transformative power that had ignited within him.

The protagonist seeks out a mentor or joins a secret organization dedicated to the Falcon's cause.

Driven by his unwavering determination to follow in the Falcon's footsteps, Patrick sought guidance beyond the confines of the White Falcons. He ventured into the depths of the realm, seeking out a mentor who could further unlock his potential and connect him to the greater cause that the Falcon symbolized.

Word had reached Patrick of a secret organization known as the Brotherhood of Feathers, an elusive group dedicated to upholding justice and safeguarding the innocent. Whispers carried tales of their unwavering commitment and their deep-rooted knowledge of the Falcon's teachings.

Patrick's quest led him through hidden passages and into the heart of a clandestine meeting place. There, amidst flickering candlelight, he met with the enigmatic figure known as Master Asher. Cloaked in mystery and bearing the marks of countless battles, Master Asher possessed a wisdom that transcended the boundaries of time.

Recognizing the fire burning within Patrick's eyes, Master Asher extended his hand. "You seek the path of the Falcon, young one," he intoned, his voice carrying the weight of ages. "Within the Brotherhood of Feathers, you shall find the knowledge and training to become a guardian of justice. But remember, the path is treacherous and demands unwavering commitment."

Without hesitation, Patrick accepted the mentorship of Master Asher and embarked on a new chapter of his journey. He would learn the secrets of the Brotherhood, embracing their code and dedicating himself to the cause that had called him forth.

They undergo rigorous training, both physically and mentally, to become a skilled and formidable force.

Within the halls of the Brotherhood of Feathers, Patrick found himself immersed in a regimen of training that tested the limits of his physical and mental fortitude. Each day brought new challenges and arduous tasks designed to mold him into a skilled and formidable force.

Under the guidance of Master Asher, Patrick's training extended beyond the art of falconry. He was immersed in the intricacies of combat, honing his skills with various weapons and mastering martial techniques. Endless hours were spent perfecting his agility, speed, and strength, transforming him into a force to be reckoned with.

But the training went beyond physical prowess. Patrick delved into the depths of ancient texts, studying the history of the Falcon and the principles that guided the Brotherhood. He learned to harness his inner focus, cultivating a clarity of mind that allowed him to perceive the subtle nuances of his surroundings.

Days turned into weeks, weeks into months, as Patrick's body and mind underwent a profound transformation. He embraced the discipline demanded of him, surrendering to the relentless pursuit of excellence. With each new challenge conquered, his confidence grew, and he felt the power of the Falcon's teachings flowing through his veins.

The protagonist's transformation from an ordinary individual to a confident and capable hero is explored.

Throughout his training, Patrick's transformation from an ordinary individual to a confident and capable hero became increasingly apparent. Gone was the uncertainty that had once plagued him, replaced by a quiet confidence and an unyielding determination to uphold justice.

His once-shaky steps had become sure and purposeful, each movement imbued with grace and precision. The doubts that had once clouded his mind were replaced by a resolute focus, allowing him to navigate the complexities of his training with unwavering resolve.

As Patrick honed his physical skills, he also delved deeper into the realms of self-discovery and inner strength. He confronted his fears, faced his own weaknesses, and emerged victorious. The fire within him burned brighter than ever, fueled by the teachings of the Falcon and the guidance of Master Asher.

The transformation within Patrick was not limited to his physical prowess or mental acuity. It extended to the depths of his character and the essence of his being. He had evolved into a beacon of hope, embodying the ideals of justice, compassion, and unwavering dedication to the cause he had embraced.

Through the crucible of rigorous training, Patrick had shed the skin of his former self. He emerged as a hero in the making, ready to take flight and face the challenges that awaited him. The ordinary individual he once was had been replaced by a confident and capable force, driven by the call of the Falcon and fueled by a sense of purpose that would guide him on his destined path.

Chapter 3: Training and Transformation

In the realm of the White Falcons, the air crackled with anticipation as Patrick delved deeper into his training. The walls of the ancient training ground echoed with the fluttering of wings and the whispers of knowledge passed down through generations. It was within these hallowed halls that Patrick would undergo a metamorphosis, both physically and spiritually.

Under the watchful eye of Elder Farin, Patrick immersed himself in the rigors of falconry. From dawn till dusk, he sparred with his avian companions, honing his reflexes, and sharpening his senses. His body became an extension of the falcon's grace, his movements fluid and precise.

But the training extended far beyond physical prowess. Elder Farin recognized that true power lay not only in the strength of the body but also in the depths of the mind and the purity of the spirit. Patrick was taught the ancient ways of connecting with the falcons on a profound level, delving into the realms of telepathy and empathy, forging a bond that transcended the boundaries of the physical.

Days turned into weeks, and weeks into months as Patrick absorbed the wisdom imparted by his mentor. The falcons became his companions, their keen intellect guiding him on a path of self-discovery.

Through their eyes, he witnessed the world from a different perspective, a perspective that demanded both vigilance and compassion.

As Patrick trained, a transformation unfolded within him. He shed the uncertainty that had once plagued his steps, replacing it with unwavering confidence and a heightened awareness of the world around him. His senses became keener, his intuition sharper. He could discern the hidden truths that lay beneath the surface, sensing the intentions of others and unraveling the webs of deception.

Yet, it was not only his skills that underwent a transformation. Patrick 's spirit blossomed, infused with the virtues of the Falcon. He became a beacon of hope, a source of inspiration for his fellow White Falcons and those who witnessed his dedication.

They saw in him the embodiment of the legends, a reminder that righteousness and courage could triumph over the darkest of adversities.

In the stillness of the night, as Patrick communed with his falcon companion, he felt the weight of his purpose settle upon him. The training had not only shaped his abilities but also instilled within him a profound understanding of his role in the world. He was destined to be a guardian, a protector of the innocent, and a symbol of justice.

With newfound clarity, Patrick emerged from his training, ready to face the challenges that awaited him beyond the walls of the White Falcons' domain. His transformation was not only physical but also a testament to his unwavering resolve to fight for what was right, to follow the path set before him by the Falcon and the mysterious encounter that had changed his life.

The time had come for Patrick to spread his wings and soar beyond the sheltered embrace of his training ground. The world awaited, its complexities and perils ready to test his mettle. He was no longer the wide- eyed novice but a warrior, emboldened by his training and infused with the spirit of the Falcon.

And so, with his falcon companion by his side, Patrick embarked on the next chapter of his journey, the echoes of his training reverberating within him. The trials would be arduous, and the path ahead uncertain, but his transformation had equipped him with the strength and wisdom to navigate the challenges that lay ahead.

As the sun dipped below the horizon, Patrick spread his wings, ready to soar into the unknown. The world awaited its champion, its guardian of justice and hope. And Patrick , armed with his falcon and the teachings of the White Falcons, would rise to meet the challenges head-on, embracing the transformative power that had ignited within him.

A. The protagonist seeks out a mentor or joins a secret organization dedicated to the Falcon's cause.

Driven by his unwavering determination to follow in the Falcon's footsteps, Patrick sought guidance beyond the confines of the White Falcons. He ventured into the depths of the realm, seeking out a mentor who could further unlock his potential and connect him to the greater cause that the Falcon symbolized.

Word had reached Patrick of a secret organization known as the Brotherhood of Feathers, an elusive group dedicated to upholding justice and safeguarding the innocent. Whispers carried tales of their unwavering commitment and their deep-rooted knowledge of the Falcon's teachings.

Patrick 's quest led him through hidden passages and into the heart of a clandestine meeting place. There, amidst flickering candlelight, he met with the enigmatic figure known as Master Asher. Cloaked in mystery and bearing the marks of countless battles, Master Asher possessed a wisdom that transcended the boundaries of time.

Recognizing the fire burning within Patrick 's eyes, Master Asher extended his hand. "You seek the path of the Falcon, young one," he intoned, his voice carrying the weight of ages. "Within the Brotherhood of Feathers, you shall find the knowledge and training to become a guardian of justice. But remember, the path is treacherous and demands unwavering commitment."

Without hesitation, Patrick accepted the mentorship of Master Asher and embarked on a new chapter of his journey. He would learn the secrets of the Brotherhood, embracing their code and dedicating himself to the cause that had called him forth.

A. They undergo rigorous training, both physically and mentally, to become a skilled and formidable force.

Within the halls of the Brotherhood of Feathers, Patrick found himself immersed in a regimen of training that tested the limits of his physical and mental fortitude. Each day brought new challenges and arduous tasks designed to mold him into a skilled and formidable force.

Under the guidance of Master Asher, Patrick 's training extended beyond the art of falconry. He was immersed in the intricacies of combat, honing his skills with various weapons and mastering martial techniques. Endless hours were spent perfecting his agility, speed, and strength, transforming him into a force to be reckoned with.

But the training went beyond physical prowess. Patrick delved into the depths of ancient texts, studying the history of the Falcon and the principles that guided the Brotherhood. He learned to harness his inner focus, cultivating a clarity of mind that allowed him to perceive the subtle nuances of his surroundings.

Days turned into weeks, weeks into months, as Patrick 's body and mind underwent a profound transformation. He embraced the discipline demanded of him, surrendering to the relentless pursuit of excellence. With each new challenge conquered, his confidence grew, and he felt the power of the Falcon's teachings flowing through his veins.

A. The protagonist's transformation from an ordinary individual to a confident and capable hero is explored.

Throughout his training, Patrick 's transformation from an ordinary individual to a confident and capable hero became increasingly apparent. Gone was the uncertainty that had once plagued him, replaced by a quiet confidence and an unyielding determination to uphold justice.

His once-shaky steps had become sure and purposeful, each movement imbued with grace and precision. The doubts that had once clouded his mind were replaced by a resolute focus, allowing him to navigate the complexities of his training with unwavering resolve.

As Patrick honed his physical skills, he also delved deeper into the realms of self-discovery and inner strength. He confronted his fears, faced his own weaknesses, and emerged victorious. The fire within him burned brighter than ever, fueled by the teachings of the Falcon and the guidance of Master Asher.

The transformation within Patrick was not limited to his physical prowess or mental acuity. It extended to the depths of his character and the essence of his being. He had evolved into a beacon of hope, embodying the ideals of justice, compassion, and unwavering dedication to the cause he had embraced.

Through the crucible of rigorous training, Patrick had shed the skin of his former self. He emerged as a hero in the making, ready to take flight and face the challenges that awaited him. The ordinary individual he once was had been replaced by a confident and capable force, driven by the call of the Falcon and fueled by a sense of purpose that would guide him on his destined path.

Chapter 4: Rising Threats

As Patrick's training with the Brotherhood of Feathers reached its zenith, a sense of unease settled upon the land. Whispers carried on the wind, speaking of rising threats that loomed on the horizon. The delicate balance between order and chaos was tilting, and the world cried out for its heroes to rise.

Word reached Patrick of a clandestine alliance known as the Shadow Wing, a group fueled by dark ambitions and driven by a hunger for power. Their ranks swelled with renegades and mercenaries, united by a shared disdain for the principles of justice and compassion.

The Brotherhood of Feathers, recognizing the urgency of the situation, summoned Patrick and his fellow warriors to a gathering in the heart of their sanctum. There, Master Asher addressed the assembly, his voice resonating with steely resolve.

"Our world faces a perilous threat," Master Asher proclaimed, his eyes scanning the faces of the assembled Brotherhood members. "The Shadow Wing seeks to plunge us into darkness, to tear asunder the fabric of harmony that we have sworn to protect. We must stand as a united front against this rising tide of tyranny."

Patrick's heart burned with determination as he absorbed the weight of Master Asher's words. The call to action reverberated within him, fueling the fire of justice that burned in his soul. He knew that he must rise to meet the challenges ahead, to confront the rising threats that threatened to consume the world.

Guided by the wisdom of the Brotherhood, Patrick and his comrades embarked on a series of missions, their purpose twofold: to gather intelligence on the Shadow Wing's activities and to disrupt their nefarious plans. Each mission tested their mettle, pushing them to the brink of their abilities and calling upon their unwavering loyalty to the cause.

As they infiltrated hidden lairs and engaged in covert operations, Patrick witnessed firsthand the extent of the Shadow Wing's reach. Their agents, skilled and ruthless, moved like phantoms in the night, spreading fear and chaos in their wake. The stakes grew higher with each encounter, as the Shadow Wing revealed their true intentions - to seize control, to subjugate the innocent, and to extinguish the flickering flames of hope.

In the face of mounting adversity, Patrick's transformation into a formidable warrior proved invaluable. His training with the Brotherhood had honed his skills to a razor's edge, enabling him to face the Shadow Wing's forces with confidence and strategic prowess. He fought alongside his brothers and sisters in arms, their unity a testament to the strength of their cause.

With every victory won, Patrick's resolve deepened. The threats that once seemed insurmountable now became opportunities for him to prove his worth, to defend the ideals he held dear. He stood as a symbol of hope amidst the encroaching darkness, inspiring his comrades and instilling fear in the hearts of those who sought to sow chaos.

But as the rising threats tested their resolve, Patrick knew that the battle had only just begun. The Shadow Wing's grip tightened, their influence reaching further into the world. It was clear that a cataclysmic clash between light and dark loomed on the horizon, a confrontation that would determine the fate of all.

And so, with steely determination, Patrick and the Brotherhood of Feathers braced themselves for the battles to come. The rising threats would not deter them, for they stood united in their mission to safeguard justice, to protect the innocent, and to confront the darkness that threatened to engulf their world. With their falcons soaring above them, their spirits aflame with purpose, they stood poised to face whatever awaited them, ready to rise against the oncoming storm.

powerful villain or organization emerges, threatening peace and stability.

As the shadow of the Shadow Wing grew darker, a powerful villain emerged from their ranks, a figure who personified the malevolence that had gripped the land. Known only as Lord Malachi, he exuded an aura of dark charisma and commanded the loyalty of his subordinates with an iron fist. Lord Malachi's ultimate goal was nothing short of domination, seeking to dismantle the foundations of peace and stability that had been painstakingly built.

With every passing day, the Shadow Wing's influence spread like a poisonous vine, ensnaring the hearts and minds of the desperate and disillusioned. Their acts of cruelty and oppression left scars upon the land, and the innocent suffered under their merciless reign.

The Falcon's legacy and the protagonist's involvement attract the attention of the antagonist.

News of the protagonist's training with the Brotherhood of Feathers and his connection to the Falcon's legacy did not go unnoticed by Lord Malachi. The antagonist's piercing eyes, filled with malice, fixated upon Patrick as an embodiment of resistance and a threat to his nefarious plans.

Enraged by the defiance that Patrick and his comrades represented, Lord Malachi set his sights on eradicating the last remnants of hope. He sought to crush the Falcon's legacy, viewing it as a beacon that could rally the forces against him. The clash between Patrick's unwavering determination and Lord Malachi's thirst for power was inevitable, their paths destined to intersect in a battle that would shake the foundations of their world.

The protagonist faces initial challenges and setbacks while uncovering the villain's plans.

As Patrick delved deeper into his quest to thwart the Shadow Wing and their malevolent leader, he faced a series of initial challenges and setbacks. Lord Malachi's web of deception was far-reaching, entangling unsuspecting individuals and weaving intricate plots that masked his true intentions.

Patrick's journey to uncover the villain's plans was rife with obstacles. He encountered spies and traps, their purpose to hinder his progress and sow doubt within his heart. The initial setbacks threatened to dampen his spirit, but Patrick's unwavering determination burned brighter than ever.

With each setback, Patrick grew more resolute. He called upon the wisdom of his mentors, the teachings of the Falcon, and the bond he shared with his falcon companion to navigate the treacherous path laid before him. His unwavering spirit refused to yield in the face of adversity, for he understood that setbacks were merely stepping stones toward ultimate victory.

As Patrick unraveled the layers of Lord Malachi's schemes, a clearer picture emerged. The antagonist's plans extended far beyond personal gain; they struck at the heart of the values Patrick held dear. He witnessed the suffering inflicted upon innocent lives, the destruction wrought upon lands once filled with joy and prosperity.

The challenges and setbacks only fueled Patrick's determination. With renewed purpose, he redoubled his efforts to expose Lord Malachi's malevolence and bring an end to the reign of darkness. Patrick knew that the road ahead would be perilous, with the weight of his responsibility resting squarely on his shoulders. But he also knew that he would not waver, for the Falcon's legacy and the very hope of the world depended on his unwavering resolve.

Chapter 5: Alliance and Betrayal

The echoes of Lord Malachi's tyranny reverberated through the land, driving Patrick to seek out allies in his quest to dismantle the Shadow Wing's hold. He knew that he could not face the powerful adversary alone, and that unity would be the key to their success.

In his pursuit of like-minded individuals, Patrick encountered a group known as the Crimson Talons, fierce warriors whose skills were legendary. Led by the indomitable Captain Aria, they had long fought against injustice and oppression, their reputation preceding them.

With humility and determination, Patrick approached Captain Aria, sharing the tales of Lord Malachi's atrocities and the threat posed by the Shadow Wing. Recognizing the gravity of the situation, Captain Aria and her warriors pledged their swords to the cause, their shared goal to bring an end to the reign of darkness.

The alliance between the Brotherhood of Feathers and the Crimson Talons marked a turning point in the battle against the Shadow Wing. Their combined strength, skill, and unwavering determination created a force that struck fear into the hearts of their enemies.

Yet, amidst the alliance, whispers of betrayal loomed. Doubt cast a shadow on the unity they had forged, and Patrick sensed a fracture within their ranks. He knew that trust, the very foundation of their alliance, must be safeguarded at all costs.

It became apparent that a traitor lurked within their midst, feeding information to Lord Malachi and jeopardizing their plans. Patrick and Captain Aria, united by their determination to weed out the betrayer, embarked on a treacherous journey of investigation and subterfuge.

As they unraveled the web of deception, shocking revelations came to light. A member of their own ranks had succumbed to the allure of power and had been swayed by Lord Malachi's promises. The traitor's actions had led to the loss of valuable lives and compromised their every move.

Betrayal tore at the fabric of their alliance, threatening to fracture the unity they had fought so hard to forge. Patrick and Captain Aria were faced with a difficult decision - to cast aside the traitor and sever the poisoned branch, or to seek redemption and give the betrayer an opportunity for redemption.

With heavy hearts and the weight of justice on their shoulders, Patrick and Captain Aria confronted the traitor. Their resolve was unyielding, for they knew that their cause demanded uncompromising integrity. The fate of the alliance and the future of their world hung in the balance.

The betrayer, faced with the consequences of their actions, pleaded for forgiveness, their voice tinged with remorse. Patrick and Captain Aria stood as judges, weighing the scales of justice against the potential for redemption. In the end, they made their decision, guided by their unwavering commitment to their cause.

The alliance weathered the storm of betrayal, emerging stronger and more resolute. The Crimson Talons and the Brotherhood of Feathers united as one, their trust and loyalty renewed. The betrayal had served as a stark reminder of the stakes they faced, reinvigorating their determination to vanquish Lord Malachi and restore peace to their world.

With their ranks solidified, Patrick, Captain Aria, and their combined forces set their sights on their ultimate goal. The battles that awaited them would be fierce and demanding, but the alliance they had formed would prove unbreakable. The path ahead was treacherous, but they would face it together, united in their purpose and unwavering in their resolve to bring an end to Lord Malachi's reign.

As the sun set on the eve of their most challenging confrontation yet, Patrick and his allies stood shoulder to shoulder, their hearts aflame with determination.

They knew that the road ahead would test their limits, but their alliance would serve as an unyielding bastion against the forces of darkness.

In the face of Lord Malachi's wrath and the lingering specter of betrayal, Patrick and his newfound allies were prepared to march into battle, ready to confront their destinies head-on. The battle lines were drawn, and the world held its breath, waiting for the clash that would determine the fate of all.

The protagonist forms alliances with other individuals who share the same goal.

In the face of Lord Malachi's rising threat, Patrick recognized the need to form alliances with other individuals who shared a common goal: to dismantle the Shadow Wing and restore peace to their land. He sought out like-minded warriors, individuals whose resolve burned as brightly as his own.

Through his journeys, Patrick encountered a diverse group of allies, each possessing unique skills and experiences. Some had personal vendettas against the Shadow Wing, while others simply yearned for a world free from tyranny. They came from different walks of life, but their shared purpose united them.

With a firm handshake and a shared understanding, Patrick forged alliances with these individuals. Their shared determination and complementary abilities created a formidable force, ready to face the challenges that lay ahead. Bound by a common cause, they pledged to fight side by side, drawing strength from one another.

A traitor is revealed within the protagonist's circle, creating a sense of mistrust and danger.

As the alliance grew stronger, a sinister undercurrent of mistrust began to surface. Whispers reached Patrick's ears, hinting at the presence of a traitor within their midst. Suspicion cast a shadow over their once-unified ranks, threatening to sow discord and undermine their collective efforts.

With trepidation and a heavy heart, Patrick delved into the depths of their ranks, determined to uncover the truth. The discovery of a traitor created a rift in their unity, igniting fear and suspicion among the once-trusted allies. The very foundation of their alliance seemed to crumble as doubts infiltrated their thoughts and hearts.

The protagonist must navigate the complexities of loyalty and betrayal while keeping their mission alive.

Caught in the crosscurrents of loyalty and betrayal, Patrick found himself navigating treacherous waters. The revelation of a traitor threatened to dismantle the fragile trust they had built, leaving the alliance vulnerable and their mission in jeopardy. The weight of their purpose pressed upon Patrick's shoulders as he sought to uphold justice while dealing with the betrayal within their ranks.

In the face of this newfound danger, Patrick had to tread carefully, separating friend from foe and determining who could still be trusted. The complexities of loyalty and betrayal weaved a web of uncertainty, making it difficult to discern truth from deception. Yet, Patrick understood that to succeed, they must overcome the sense of mistrust that threatened to tear them apart.

With resilience and unwavering determination, Patrick navigated the challenges that loyalty and betrayal presented. He relied on his instincts and the counsel of his most trusted allies to uncover the truth and separate those still dedicated to the cause from the turncoat in their midst.

As Patrick confronted the traitor, he faced a choice that would shape the course of their mission. With measured judgment and the weight of justice upon him, Patrick made a decision that sought to preserve the alliance's integrity and ensure the success of their mission. It was a test of his leadership and unwavering commitment to their cause.

The journey forward would be fraught with danger, for the scars of betrayal ran deep. Patrick and his remaining allies knew that their mission demanded vigilance and unity. They would hold each other accountable, their shared purpose acting as a beacon in the face of darkness.

In the midst of the complexities of loyalty and betrayal, Patrick remained steadfast. He would not allow the actions of a traitor to erode their collective determination. With renewed resolve, he rallied his loyal allies, reinforcing their commitment to one another and the mission that had brought them together.

Together, they would overcome the sense of mistrust, rise above the dangers of betrayal, and continue their march towards justice. The path ahead was fraught with peril, but their shared purpose burned brighter than ever. The mission remained alive, fueled by the resilience of their alliance and Patrick's unyielding commitment to see it through to the end.

Chapter 6: Climactic Battle

The time had come for the climactic battle that would determine the fate of their world. Patrick, alongside his trusted allies and the united forces of the Brotherhood of Feathers and the Crimson Talons, stood at the precipice of their final confrontation with Lord Malachi and his Shadow Wing.

The battlefield lay shrouded in darkness, an eerie silence hanging heavy in the air. The clash of swords and the roar of battle loomed as an imminent storm. Patrick's heart beat in harmony with the pulse of anticipation, his every fiber alive with the knowledge that this was the moment they had prepared for.

The forces of light and darkness collided with an explosive fury, the clash of steel reverberating through the air. Patrick led his allies with unwavering resolve, his falcon companion soaring above, guiding him through the chaos. Their unity, forged through hardship and shared purpose, was their greatest weapon against Lord Malachi's malevolence.

The battlefield became a maelstrom of magic and combat, the forces of justice clashing with the minions of darkness. Patrick's allies fought with courage and tenacity, their determination aflame with the knowledge that they were the last defense against Lord Malachi's reign of terror.

Amidst the chaos, Patrick locked eyes with Lord Malachi, their gazes an unspoken challenge. The antagonist exuded a sinister aura, his power unmatched but not unassailable. Patrick felt the

weight of their destinies converging, their clash a culmination of all they had fought for.

With every strike, Patrick drew upon the training and guidance he had received. His movements were fluid and precise, a testament to his transformation from an ordinary individual to a confident and capable hero.

The teachings of the Falcon, the resilience of his allies, and his unwavering resolve fueled his every action.

As the battle raged on, Patrick's allies fought with unwavering determination, their spirits undeterred by the overwhelming odds. Each clash of swords, each burst of magic, brought them closer to victory or defeat. Their unity proved to be their greatest strength, as they stood as a beacon of hope against the encroaching darkness.

The climactic battle was a symphony of chaos and valor, as warriors on both sides demonstrated their unwavering loyalty to their cause. The clash between light and darkness intensified, the very fabric of their world hanging in the balance.

In the midst of the chaos, Patrick found himself face- to-face with Lord Malachi. Their clash became a dance of opposing forces, each strike carrying the weight of their convictions. Patrick's determination burned brighter than ever, fueled by the legacy of the Falcon and the sacrifices made by those who believed in him.

As the battle reached its crescendo, Patrick's resolve surged. He called upon the combined strength and unity of his allies, their shared purpose intertwining like threads of fate. Their collective power became an unstoppable force, surging forth with unwavering resolve.

In a final, climactic clash, Patrick and Lord Malachi clashed with the force of titans. The clash of steel reverberated through the air, the ground trembling beneath their feet. Sparks flew as their powers collided, each refusing to yield to the other.

With a resolute determination, Patrick channeled the spirit of the Falcon within him, unleashing a surge of power that engulfed Lord Malachi. The darkness receded, consumed by the overwhelming light of justice and righteousness.

In the aftermath of the climactic battle, Patrick and his allies stood triumphant. Lord Malachi lay defeated, his grip on power shattered. The world basked in a newfound peace, the shadow of the Shadow Wing dissipating like mist at dawn.

But the battle had exacted a toll. The sacrifices made by Patrick and his allies were etched into their hearts, a reminder of the cost of their victory. They mourned the fallen, honoring their memory and vowing to protect the fragile peace they had fought so hard to achieve.

As the dust settled, Patrick's gaze turned towards the horizon, a new dawn breaking. The world lay before him, forever changed by their efforts. The Falcon's legacy lived on in their hearts, a symbol of hope and justice that would guide future generations.

With their mission accomplished, Patrick and his comrades looked towards the future, knowing that their heroism would forever be etched into the annals of their world's history. They had weathered the storm, faced their darkest fears, and emerged as champions of light.

And so, with the echoes of the climactic battle still ringing in their ears, Patrick and his allies embarked on the next chapter of their lives. They carried with them the indomitable spirit of the Falcon, their hearts filled with hope and the knowledge that together, they could overcome any challenge that dared to threaten their world's peace.

The stakes escalate as the protagonist uncovers the full extent of the villain's plot.

As the climactic battle loomed, the full extent of Lord Malachi's plot was revealed, sending shockwaves through Patrick and his allies. The stakes escalated to unimaginable heights as they uncovered the depths of the antagonist's malevolence.

Through painstaking investigation and unwavering resolve, Patrick unearthed Lord Malachi's grand design—a plan to unleash chaos and destruction upon the world. The scale of the threat was far greater than they had anticipated, a cataclysmic scheme that would shatter the very foundations of peace and stability.

The realization fueled Patrick's determination, intensifying the fire within him to thwart Lord Malachi's plot at all costs. With every new revelation, their resolve solidified, their hearts aflame with the knowledge that failure was not an option. The fate of their world hung in the balance, driving them to fight with unwavering purpose.

The Falcon and the protagonist unite forces to confront the antagonist in an epic showdown.

As the battle reached its climax, the Falcon, a legendary figure and embodiment of justice, emerged from the shadows. The legendary hero sensed the urgency of the situation and joined forces with Patrick, their shared purpose binding them together.

The union of the Falcon and Patrick, the torchbearers of hope and righteousness, was a symbol of unwavering determination. Together, they stood as the embodiment of the cause they fought for—the epitome of justice and the antithesis of Lord Malachi's malevolence.

The epic showdown between the united forces of the Falcon and Patrick against Lord Malachi became the defining moment of their struggle. The clash of powers and ideologies reverberated through the battlefield, as the forces of light and darkness collided in an elemental battle for the fate of their world.

The battle tests the protagonist's skills, determination, and belief in the Falcon's cause.

In the crucible of the climactic battle, Patrick's skills, determination, and unwavering belief in the Falcon's cause were put to the ultimate test. Every fiber of his being was pushed to the limit as he confronted Lord Malachi's formidable powers and relentless minions.

The battle demanded not only physical prowess but also mental fortitude. Patrick drew upon the training and teachings he had received, his every move guided by the wisdom of the Falcon. His skills honed through trials and hardships were unleashed in a display of mastery and resilience.

Amidst the chaos and desperation, doubts and moments of faltering belief assailed Patrick. The weight of the world's hopes and the enormity of the task before him threatened to overwhelm his spirit. Yet, in those moments of darkness, the Falcon's legacy shone brightly, igniting a renewed determination within him.

Patrick's belief in the cause he fought for, the unwavering faith in the Falcon's guidance, propelled him forward. He summoned the depths of his strength and unleashed a torrent of bravery and determination that eclipsed any doubts that sought to plague his mind.

The battle became a testament to Patrick's growth and transformation. It tested not only his physical and magical abilities but also his resolve and belief in the Falcon's cause. With each blow exchanged and each spell cast, Patrick's conviction burned brighter, driving him to surpass his limits and confront the darkness that threatened to engulf their world.

In the climax of the battle, Patrick's unwavering determination and belief in the Falcon's cause bore fruit. The culmination of his skills, the strength of his allies, and the legacy of the Falcon converged in a final, decisive strike against Lord Malachi.

With a resounding clash of powers, Patrick's victory became a resolute declaration of justice prevailing over tyranny. The battle-tested hero stood tall amidst the chaos, his spirit unyielding, and his commitment to the Falcon's cause unshakable.

As the dust settled and peace returned to their land, Patrick and the Falcon, their united forces victorious, knew that their battle was not in vain. The trials they had endured had shaped them into exemplars of hope and champions of justice.

With hearts aflame with triumph and a world forever changed by their efforts, Patrick and the Falcon shared a moment of gratitude and reflection. The climactic battle had tested them in ways unimaginable, but their shared purpose and unwavering belief in the Falcon's cause had carried them to victory.

Their alliance had forged a legacy that would endure through generations, inspiring future heroes to rise against the forces of darkness. Patrick, forever changed by his journey, carried the Falcon's spirit within him as a guiding light, a beacon of hope for a world that would always face new challenges.

And so, with the battle won and the dawn of a new era upon them, Patrick and the Falcon stood side by side, ready to face whatever trials awaited them in the future. The world had been transformed, and they, bound by their shared legacy, were prepared to embrace the challenges of a brighter, more just tomorrow.

Chapter 7: Redemption and Legacy

With the climactic battle won and the forces of darkness vanquished, a sense of tranquility settled upon the land. Patrick, the Falcon, and their allies stood as beacons of hope, their victory serving as a catalyst for redemption and the establishment of a lasting legacy.

In the aftermath of the battle, the realm grappled with the aftermath of Lord Malachi's reign. The scars of his tyranny ran deep, leaving communities shattered and hearts burdened with grief. It was a time of healing and rebuilding, a chance for redemption to flourish in the wake of darkness.

Patrick and his allies, understanding the weight of their responsibility, dedicated themselves to the arduous task of mending what had been broken. They worked tirelessly, extending compassion and aid to those affected by the Shadow Wing's reign. Their acts of kindness and selflessness became the foundation upon which a new era of unity and harmony was built.

As they traveled through the war-torn regions, Patrick witnessed firsthand the transformative power of redemption. Former followers of the Shadow Wing, disillusioned and remorseful, sought solace in the newfound hope that radiated from the victorious heroes. They yearned for redemption, and Patrick, embodying the spirit of forgiveness, offered them a chance to rebuild their lives and contribute to the restoration of their world.

The path to redemption was not without challenges. Lingering doubts and resentments threatened to

hinder the healing process. But through empathy, understanding, and unwavering belief in the potential for change, Patrick and his allies helped guide the wayward souls towards a brighter path.

The Falcon, too, played a pivotal role in the redemption of the realm. Their wisdom and guidance became a beacon of light, inspiring others to rise above their past mistakes and embrace the opportunity for a fresh start. The legacy of the Falcon grew, not only as a symbol of justice but also as a testament to the power of redemption and the capacity for growth within every individual.

As the realm slowly healed, Patrick reflected upon the legacy he had become a part of. The lessons learned, the bonds forged, and the trials overcome would forever shape the narrative of their world. The stories of heroism and redemption would be passed down through generations, inspiring future heroes to rise and confront the challenges that would inevitably arise.

With humility and gratitude, Patrick accepted his role as a custodian of the Falcon's legacy. He understood that the battles fought and the sacrifices made were not in vain. Their triumph over darkness had paved the way for a brighter future—a future built on compassion, unity, and the unwavering pursuit of justice.

In the years that followed, Patrick continued to champion the cause he had fought so fiercely for. He became a mentor and guide, passing on the teachings of the Falcon to the next generation of heroes. His legacy, intertwined with that of the Falcon, would endure as a testament to the power of belief, the strength of unity, and the redemptive potential within every individual.

As Patrick walked the path of redemption and legacy, he knew that the journey was never truly over. The world would always face new challenges, new villains waiting to rise. But with the Falcon's teachings and the indomitable spirit of redemption as their guide, Patrick and his successors would forever stand ready to confront the darkness and usher in a brighter, more just tomorrow.

And so, as the sun set on their realm, Patrick took solace in the knowledge that he had played a part in shaping a legacy that would endure for eternity. The Falcon's call had awakened a hero within him, and his journey had been one of transformation, redemption, and the forging of a legacy that would forever be etched in the annals of their world's history.

The protagonist triumphs over the antagonist, but not without sacrifice.

The final confrontation with Lord Malachi reached its climactic peak, and Patrick faced his nemesis with unwavering resolve. In a battle that shook the very foundations of their world, Patrick triumphed over the forces of darkness, ensuring that justice prevailed.

However, the victory came at a cost. Sacrifices had been made, lives lost in the struggle against Lord Malachi's tyranny. Patrick felt the weight of their absence, their memories forever etched in his heart. The sacrifices made by those who believed in the cause added a bittersweet layer to the triumph, a reminder of the price paid for their hard-fought victory.

The Falcon's legacy is solidified through the protagonist's actions and their impact on the world.

Patrick's actions and unwavering belief in the Falcon's cause solidified the legacy of the legendary hero.

Through their triumph over Lord Malachi and the redemption they brought to the realm, the Falcon's legacy became a beacon of inspiration and hope for generations to come.

The impact of Patrick's deeds reverberated throughout the world, their echoes a reminder of the power of justice, compassion, and the unwavering pursuit of righteousness. The Falcon's name became synonymous with courage and virtue, their story interwoven with Patrick's own.

The world, forever changed by their actions, began to rebuild and heal. The Falcon's legacy became a cornerstone upon which a new era of unity, compassion, and harmony could be built. Patrick's impact on the world ensured that the Falcon's spirit would endure, a guiding light for future heroes to follow.

The protagonist reflects on their journey and the lessons learned, setting the stage for potential sequels.

As the dust settled and peace settled upon the realm, Patrick took a moment to reflect on the incredible journey that had brought him to this point. He contemplated the lessons learned, the challenges faced, and the growth he had undergone.

The hardships and triumphs had shaped Patrick into the hero he had become. He recognized the importance of the values instilled in him by the Falcon—the importance of empathy, unity, and the unwavering pursuit of justice. These lessons would forever guide him, serving as a compass for the future.

Patrick's reflection also set the stage for potential sequels, hinting at the challenges that lay ahead. While Lord Malachi had been defeated, the world would always face new threats and new battles to be fought. Patrick understood that his journey was not over, that the legacy he had become a part of would require continued vigilance and determination.

With his heart full of gratitude and the spirit of the Falcon burning within him, Patrick prepared himself for the future. The lessons learned, the friendships forged, and the legacy he carried would propel him forward, ready to face whatever trials awaited him.

As the sun set on this chapter of Patrick's story, a new dawn emerged—a future filled with endless possibilities, potential sequels that would delve deeper into the complexities of justice, redemption, and the ever-evolving world they inhabited. Patrick's journey had only just begun, and he stood prepared to face the challenges that awaited, carrying the legacy of the Falcon and the spirit of redemption within him.

Chapter 8: Conclusion

In the wake of victory and redemption, a sense of peace settled upon the land. Patrick, the hero who had triumphed over darkness, stood at the precipice of a new era, a chapter marked by the legacy of the Falcon and the transformative power of redemption.

The realm, once torn asunder by the malevolence of Lord Malachi and the Shadow Wing, began to rebuild with newfound hope. Communities mended what had been broken, their spirits lifted by the acts of kindness and compassion that had become the hallmark of Patrick and his allies.

Patrick, forever changed by his journey, carried the lessons learned and the memories of those lost. He recognized that true victory lay not just in defeating a formidable adversary but in healing the wounds left in their wake. He dedicated himself to the ongoing work of restoration, ensuring that the scars of the past would not define the future.

The Falcon's legacy, solidified through Patrick's actions and the impact they had on the world, permeated every aspect of their society. The ideals of justice, unity, and redemption became ingrained in the fabric of their civilization, guiding future generations towards a path of righteousness.

As Patrick looked upon the realm he had fought so hard to protect, he felt a sense of fulfillment and gratitude. The sacrifices made, the trials endured, and the unwavering belief in the Falcon's cause had led to this moment—a moment of peace and renewal.

In the years that followed, Patrick became a mentor, guiding young heroes in their own journeys of redemption and justice. The legacy of the Falcon lived on through him, a flame passed from one generation to the next, illuminating the darkness and inspiring future heroes to rise.

The conclusion of this story marked not an end, but a new beginning—a testament to the enduring power of hope, redemption, and the indomitable spirit of those who stood against the forces of darkness. Patrick's journey had taught him that heroism was not defined by one grand battle but by the everyday choices to do what was right and just.

As the realm flourished under the influence of the Falcon's legacy, Patrick took solace in knowing that his actions had made a difference. The bonds forged, the friendships kindled, and the lives touched by his unwavering resolve would forever be remembered.

In the closing chapter of this tale, Patrick stood tall, a symbol of resilience and courage. The world around him had been transformed, a testament to the power of redemption and the unwavering pursuit of justice. And though the challenges of the future remained uncertain, Patrick faced them with unwavering determination, secure in the knowledge that the Falcon's spirit would guide him and the realm towards a brighter tomorrow.

And so, with the closing of this chapter, Patrick took his final steps, his heart filled with gratitude for the incredible journey he had undertaken. The story of the Falcon rising, of redemption and legacy, would forever be etched in the annals of their world's history—a reminder that even in the darkest of times, there is always a flicker of hope, a chance for redemption, and a hero willing to answer the call.

Wrap up loose ends and provide closure for major storylines.

With the final chapter drawing to a close, loose ends were tied and major storylines found resolution. The realm, once plagued by the tyranny of Lord Malachi and the Shadow Wing, was now on the path to healing and renewal. Communities rebuilt, wounds mended, and a newfound sense of unity emerged from the ashes of the past.

Patrick and his allies, having faced their greatest challenges and triumphed over darkness, found solace in knowing that their mission had been accomplished. The realm was now free from the shackles of oppression, and the legacy of the Falcon had become an enduring symbol of hope and justice.

Hint at potential future adventures or challenges for the protagonist and the Falcon's legacy.

As the story drew to a close, whispers of potential future adventures and challenges danced in the air. Though the immediate threat had been vanquished, Patrick and the Falcon's legacy remained alive and vibrant. The world they had fought so fiercely to protect was ever-changing, and new threats and trials would inevitably arise.

Hints of future adventures lingered on the horizon, waiting to test Patrick's mettle and push the boundaries of the Falcon's legacy. The heroes who had stood united in this chapter would find themselves embarking on new journeys, facing new adversaries, and uncovering hidden secrets that threatened to unravel the fragile peace they had fought so hard to achieve.

Leave readers with a sense of hope and anticipation for what comes next.

In the final pages of this tale, readers were left with a sense of hope and anticipation. The conclusion marked not an end, but a beginning—a springboard into a future filled with untold adventures and trials.

The legacy of the Falcon, embodied in Patrick and his allies, served as a beacon of hope for a world that would always need heroes willing to stand against the forces of darkness.

As readers turned the final page, a lingering sense of anticipation hung in the air. The story had concluded, but the echoes of its impact reverberated through their hearts and minds. They were left with the belief that the heroes they had come to know and love would continue to champion justice, embarking on new journeys that would shape the fate of their world.

With a sense of hope in their hearts and the knowledge that the Falcon's legacy would endure, readers bid farewell to this chapter of the tale, eagerly anticipating the unwritten pages that awaited—pages filled with adventure, challenges, and the unwavering spirit of the Falcon rising once more.

And so, as the story reached its conclusion, the legacy of the Falcon lived on, forever etched in the hearts and minds of those who had witnessed the hero's journey. The tale of redemption and the enduring power of hope left readers with a sense of anticipation for what lay beyond—a future filled with new heroes, formidable adversaries, and the unwavering belief that justice would always prevail.

For as long as there were heroes like Patrick and the spirit of the Falcon lived on, the world would never be without hope, and the legacy of courage and redemption would endure. And so, with hearts brimming with hope and anticipation, readers closed the book, ready to embark on their own journeys of heroism and to eagerly await the tales yet to come.

Thank you and god bless you

Thank you, dear reader, for embarking on this literary journey and immersing yourself in the world of "The Falcon Rising." Your dedication and curiosity have brought the story to life, and I am grateful for the opportunity to share this tale with you.

I hope that the adventures of Patrick, the legacy of the Falcon, and the themes of redemption and hope have resonated with you. It is through your engagement and imagination that the characters and their struggles have taken on meaning and significance.

Thank you for accompanying Patrick on his quest, for embracing the triumphs and the sacrifices, and for joining in the exploration of justice, unity, and the power of redemption. Your presence as a reader has enriched the experience, and I sincerely hope that the story has left a lasting impact on your heart and mind.

May the spirit of the Falcon's legacy continue to inspire and guide you in your own journey. May it ignite within you the belief that even in the face of darkness, hope can prevail, and the strength to overcome any challenge can be found.

Once again, thank you for your time, your attention, and your dedication to "The Falcon Rising." Your readership is a gift, and I am grateful to have shared this story with you. May your future literary adventures be filled with wonder, excitement, and the profound joy of storytelling.

With heartfelt gratitude,
[Yugesh Kumar]